Stories

for

4

Year Olds

Stories for 4 Year Olds

Mandy Archer
James Newman Gray

bookoli

Contents

Crocodile's Big Adventure

Little Croc was the noisiest, fastest, bravest crocodile in the jungle.

He did super-fast tummy slides down the river.

Swoosh!

He was the first to dive into the water.

Plop! All the other crocodiles cheered and copied their friend.

While Little Croc waited for the others to take their turn, he gazed down the long river. "What is out there," he wondered, "for a brave croc like me?"

Little Croc went to the same bit of river every day.
He played with the same friends every day.
Little Croc wanted an adventure, away from his friends,
away from his family, away from his river.

"Come oh!" Little Croc's friends shouted. "Let's dive again!"

But Little Croc sneaked away.
It was time for an adventure
all of his own.

9

Little Croc walked and swam and paddled.
Soon, he was far away from home.

He spotted a family
of hippos, squelching
in the mud.

"Gross! Look at them!"
giggled Little Croc.

He tiptoed past a lion,
sleeping in the sun.
"Ssssh! Don't wake him up!"
whispered Little Croc.

He stopped to watch
parrots in the sky.
"Wow! How cool are
they?" said Little Croc.

But his friends weren't there to answer.

Little Croc looked around. He felt lonely on his own.
Then he discovered something amazing...

It was the steepest, deepest, splashiest pool
that Little Croc had ever seen!

"Wheeeeeee!"

The new pool was perfect ... and it was all his!
But Little Croc felt a bit sad.

"I miss my friends," he said.
"Playing is no fun on your own."

"Hey! Croc!"

Little Croc blinked. There were his friends!

"Why did you go?" they called.

Whee!

The crocodiles all skidded down the steep river bank.

Swoosh!

They did super-fast tummy slides.

12

Plop!

They dived into Little Croc's pool.

Little Croc felt happy and safe.
Everything felt better again, back with his family
and friends. Back where he belonged.

Who Lives Next Door?

Four little bears, in a little bear house,
each fluffy and cute and as a quiet as a mouse.

The sweet little bears: one, two, three, and four,
all have a question:

"Who's moving in next door?"

A truck parks up in the middle of the street,
excited little bears have new friends to meet!

14

A new family next door ... what a delight!
The four little bears all giggle at the sight.
The truck drives off, it's time to say hello,
a big cake is baked and around the bears go.

Four knock on the door, then they ring the bell,
but that's when they sniff a

most terrible smell...

What a foul pong! Does it come from inside?
What sort of stinky family could have arrived?

Worried little bears take a closer look,
peer in the window, then hide in a nook.

Big shadows **rattle, clatter** and go **thump!**
Every noisy crash makes the little bears **jump.**

They tiptoe round the back, quiet as mice, but someone's in the garden and they don't sound nice.

Four little bears then spot another sign, giant monster pants, blowing on the line!

The family must be **MONSTERS!** What else can they be? Monsters who gobble bears up for their tea!

The bears dash back home,
running side by side.
Bang! goes their door as
they rush inside to hide.

They stand in the hallway,
hearts all aflutter,
They turn off the light,
and pull down the shutter.

The front door opens,
the bears let out a cry ...
... a happy hippo family
have come to say 'hi'!

18

"Please excuse the stink, we love to roll in mud,
and tell us to 'sssshhhh!'
if we make a loud **thud!**"

Four little bears, they couldn't ask for more.
A friendly hippo family is living next door!

The Big Bug Ball

Down in the garden
where the long grass sways,
Creepy crawlies flutter
in the warm summer days.

Beetles and crickets,
wriggly worms and fleas.
Spiders and ladybugs,
butterflies and bees.

20

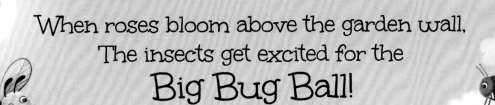

When roses bloom above the garden wall,
The insects get excited for the
Big Bug Ball!

It's a secret party under the sky.
The creatures make outfits
too small for us to spy.

Ladybug makes a skirt ready for the night,

Bee makes red
shorts ...

... Spider's cape glitters
in the light.

The creatures are happy,
and feeling bright,
Excited to show their
costumes the very
next night.

23

Poor Caterpillar has nothing to wear.

Too many legs for a suit, it would probably just tear.

Too long to wear a crinkly green leaf skirt,

She can't spin silk like Spider to make a fancy shirt.

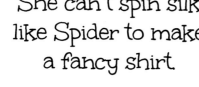

24

"I don't have a costume," Caterpillar said.

But her friends all smile and say ...

"It's time for bed."

25

Caterpillar feels sad, but she goes to sleep.

Early the next morning her friends come to have a peep.
They line up neatly, and stand by her side...

"I've changed!"

gasps Caterpillar, stretching out wide.

"I have wings to flutter, there's no need to crawl.
I've turned into a buttefly for the Big Bug Ball!"

Scaredy Dragon

Once upon a time, in a land of swirling mists, there was a dragon mountain. Most of the creatures that lived there were a blaze of shimmering scales, flicking tails, and fiery flames.

One of them was not.

Little Dragon was not like her brothers and sisters. She was a scaredy dragon.

The other dragons turned circles in the sky, but Little Dragon was too scared to fly.

The other dragons batted and clashed their tails, but Little Dragon was too worried to wrestle.

The other dragons blew burning fire, but Little Dragon was too scared to make even the tiniest puff of smoke.

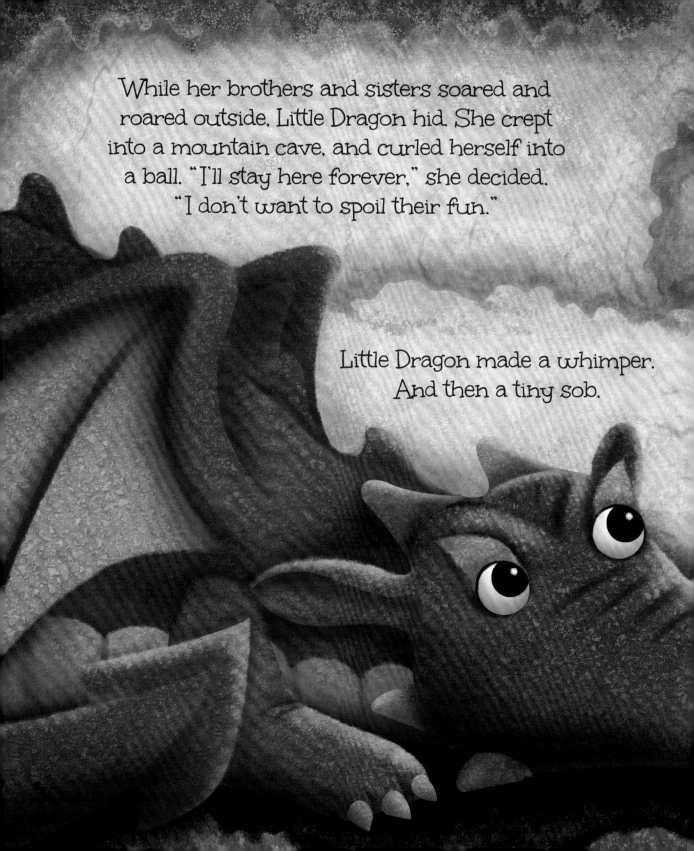

While her brothers and sisters soared and
roared outside, Little Dragon hid. She crept
into a mountain cave, and curled herself into
a ball. "I'll stay here forever," she decided.
"I don't want to spoil their fun."

Little Dragon made a whimper.
And then a tiny sob.

"I'm so alone," she sniffed.
A little voice rose out of the darkness:
"No, you're not."
Little Dragon screeched in surprise,
but there was nowhere to run.

A mouse stepped out of the shadows.

"Hello!"

Little Dragon told Mouse all about being afraid.
Mouse had a good think.

"But you are an excellent dragon," said Mouse.
"I'm worried and I'm weak," said Little Dragon.
"Not for long." Mouse leapt to his feet.
"You just have to start small."

Mouse fetched some sticks.
"Blow on these," he said.
Little Dragon did as she was told.
The sticks burst into flames,
and a little fire roared.

Poof!

"I did it!"
said Little Dragon.

Mouse found some marshmallows
to toast over the flames.
Little Dragon felt happy.

Some other dragons
noticed the fire and
came inside the cave.

"Come with us, Little Dragon!" said the
eldest dragon. "We can all fly together."

Little Dragon looked at Mouse.
"Will you come with me?"
she asked.

Mouse climbed onto Little Dragon's back.
"You can do it!" he said.
Little Dragon spread her wings, stepped off
the mountain and began to SOAR!
"I'm not a scaredy dragon!" she cried.

"I can fly!"

Mouse smiled.
"When you have a good friend,
you can do anything!"

Abracadabra!

Merlin, Soot, and Fizzibel are very special cats.

Abracadabra!
Merlin can balance
a coin on his nose.

Abracadabra!
Soot can make
himself turn blue.

Abracadabra!
Fizzibel can paint
pictures with her tail.

Merlin, Soot, and Fizzibel are witch's kittens.

There's another kitten living in the witch's shack.
Her name is Wanda. She has a white, furry tummy,
wobbly whiskers, and a tail that can't make
any sparkles at all.

Wanda is an ordinary cat.

But when Merlin's tummy is hungry,
Wanda is the first to share her supper.

Abracadabra!

"Here you go," Wanda purrs.
"There's more than enough for two."

When Soot is feeling cross,
Wanda sings a song to him.

Abracadabra!

Soot feels happy again.

And when Fizzibel tiptoes too fast along the side
of the witch's cauldron, who do you think is watching?

Plop!

"I'll save you," purrs Wanda.

Abracadabra!

Wanda pulls her friend to safety.

"Thank you, Wanda," say the kittens.
"You are the kindest kitty we know."

Wanda is no ordinary cat after all. She is extra special.
Merlin, Soot, and Fizzibel know that Wanda has
the very best magic of all ... the magic of kindness.

Planet Zed

Whoosh! A flying saucer zooms through outer space, lands on Planet Zed, then out pops a face.

Doing! A small alien lifts the bubble lid, leaps out of the saucer, landing with a skid.

42

Zoop! Off he rushes, down a deep hole, far inside a crater, spinning round a pole.

"Bloop!" says his daddy, his mama shakes her head. "It's getting late, HE MUST GO OFF TO BED!"

Whizz! Waves the alien, as he tries to flee. Mama grabs his spacesuit and sits him on her knee.

Pop! On with the pjs, squeezing in each toe. Two legs are dressed for bed, but there's still two arms to go!

44

Glug! Time for space juice, a beaker full of green.
This cheeky little alien is making quite a scene.

Zing! Brush his antenna, then watch it fizz with light.
Daddy frowns at Mama, they're in for a long night.

45

Zog! Find his cuddle moon, and how to tuck him in.
The little purple alien flashes a big grin.

Flob! Just one quick story, he's off to find a book!
Poor Mama and Daddy share a weary look.

Zip! Little purple alien, moves at lightning speed.
He climbs up to his hoverbed, ready now to read.

Zzzz! Mama? Daddy? There's no room on the bed.
He's worn them out, such noisy snores, they're fast
asleep instead!